Sunny
and
Oswaldo

Sunny
and
Oswaldo

by **Nicole Melleby**

illustrated by **Alexandra Colombo**

ALGONQUIN YOUNG READERS   2023

Published by
Algonquin Young Readers
an imprint of Workman Publishing Co., Inc.
a subsidiary of Hachette Book Group, Inc.
1290 Avenue of the Americas
New York, New York 10104

Hachette Livre, 58 rue Jean Bleuzen
92 178 Vanves Cedex, France

Hachette Book Group, UK, Carmelite House
50 Victoria Embankment, London EC4Y 0DZ

Library of Congress Cataloging-in-Publication Data

Names: Melleby, Nicole, author. | Colombo, Alexandra, illustrator.
Title: Sunny and Oswaldo / by Nicole Melleby ;
illustrated by Alexandra Colombo.
Description: First edition. | Chapel Hill, North Carolina :
Algonquin Young Readers, 2023. | Audience: Ages 4-6. | Audience:
Grades K-1. | Summary: When mean and cranky family cat
Oswaldo does not come home one day, Sunny is happy her life is
peaceful again, but when she sees how sad her dad is without him,
she soon realizes she needs to help find Oswaldo and bring
him back home.
Identifiers: LCCN 2022009321 | ISBN 9781643750958 (hardcover)
Subjects: CYAC: Cats—Fiction. | Human-animal relation-
ships—Fiction. | LCGFT: Picture books. Classification: LCC
PZ7.1.M46934 SU 2023 | DDC [E]—DC23
LC RECORD AVAILABLE AT
HTTPS://LCCN.LOC.GOV/2022009321

10 9 8 7 6 5 4 3 2 1
First Edition

For my cat, Gillian, who is a terrible cat
but a wonderful companion. —N. M.

For Massi, who chose me as *his* soulmate
and allowed me to bring him back to his
true essence. —A. C.

Sunny Swaroo did not like cats.

She especially did not like the one her dad brought home.
Sunny's dad named the cat Oswaldo.

Sunny thought it was a ridiculous name, but no one had asked for her opinion.

Fluffy would have been better—
even though the cat's fur was clumped
and matted.

Sunny thought Spots
might be good, too—
until her dad gave the cat
a bath and those spots
disappeared.

Cats were usually good at cleaning themselves.
Oswaldo wasn't a very good cat.

Oswaldo would hiss for no reason.
He would jump in Sunny's lap to steal toys.

Whenever Sunny decided to play with Oswaldo,
he decided to walk away.

Sometimes, Oswaldo would sleep all day.
Sometimes, he kept Sunny up all night.

To pet Oswaldo, Sunny would slowly, slowly
hold out her hand.
Oswaldo never let her come close.

"Leave the cat be," Sunny's mom told her.
So Sunny let Oswaldo be. She got used to his hissing.
Oswaldo would rather be with Sunny's dad, anyway.

Sunny's dad loved that cat
more than anything.

Sunny's dad laughed when Oswaldo rubbed up against his legs. He yelled when Sunny played on the floor.

If Oswaldo scratched Sunny when he got scared, her dad comforted Oswaldo. He scolded Sunny if she pushed Oswaldo away.

Sometimes Oswaldo disappeared all day.
Sunny liked the quiet when he was not there
to hiss at her.

Oswaldo always came back before bedtime.
He never hissed at her dad. He didn't need to.
Oswaldo and her dad seemed to understand
each other just fine.

Sunny hated Oswaldo.
She wished her dad had never brought him home.

One day, Oswaldo *didn't* come
back before bedtime.
Sunny was pleased.
She slept peacefully all night.

But Oswaldo didn't come home the next night, either.
Sunny's dad didn't sleep at all.

"Go help your dad look for the cat," Sunny's mom said the next morning.

"Oswaldo is old and dirty and cranky. I don't know why Dad likes him."

"He's difficult," her mom agreed. "But he's family. They need each other, Sunny."

So Sunny and her dad went looking.

When Sunny reached for her dad's hand, she reached
as slowly as she would for Oswaldo.

"Oswaldo is mean," Sunny said. "He's not a good cat."

"He was abandoned," her dad said. "He was alone and scared. Sometimes, that makes him sad. Sometimes, that makes him angry. Sometimes, that makes him want to be alone."

"That doesn't mean he's not a good cat.
That doesn't mean we shouldn't love him."

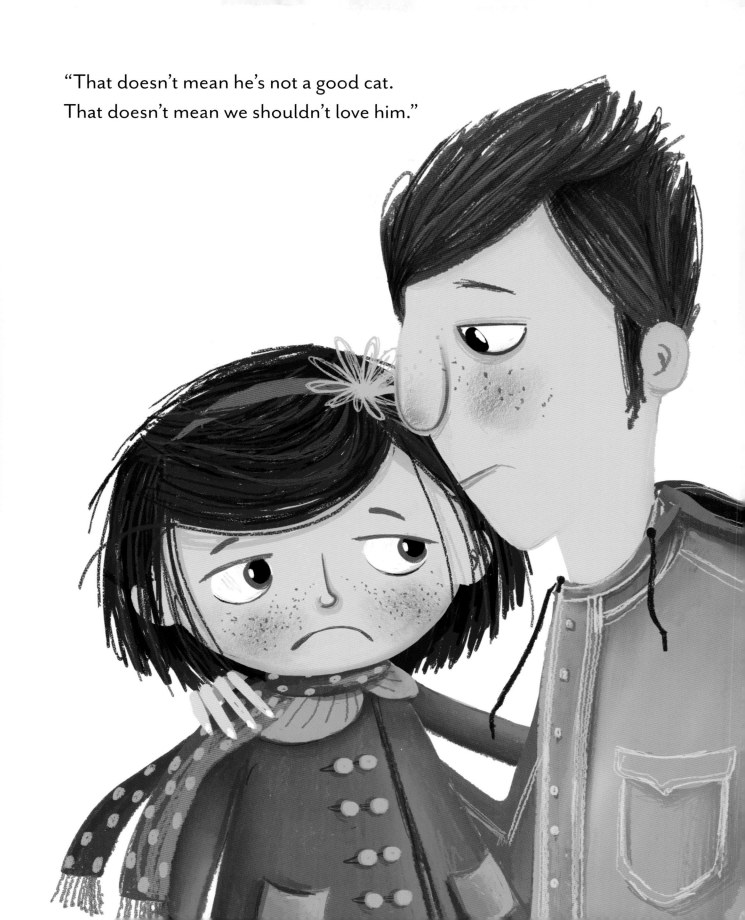

Sunny's dad sighed. "We should go back."
Sunny held tight to her dad's hand.
She thought he might cry.
She didn't want him to cry.
She didn't want Oswaldo to be sad, angry, or alone, either.
"I hope he comes home," she said.

When Sunny and her dad got home, there
was Oswaldo, on the stoop.

He was waiting, as if Sunny and her dad were
the ones who had disappeared.

Oswaldo purred as Sunny's dad picked him up.
He purred as Sunny petted him.
Sunny felt like she might start purring, too.

That night, even as her dad held tight to Oswaldo, ignoring his scruffy fur, he never let go of Sunny's hand.

Oswaldo was still purring when he
curled up between them and fell asleep.